For Nicholas, who
couldn't talk yet
—J.M.

For Scott and Peter
and my "little" brother, Jim
—L.R.

I Can't Talk Yet, but When I Do . . .

by Julie Markes

illustrated by Laura Rader

HarperCollinsPublishers

I can't talk yet, but when I do,
I'll say thank you for helping to take care of me.

I'll thank you for sharing your toys
and for making me laugh

and for helping me when I was learning to walk.

I'll say thanks for keeping me company in the backseat and for giving me licks of your ice cream cone.

When I can talk, I'll say thank you for watching out for me

and for not letting me put sand in my mouth.

When I can talk, I'll tell you how much fun I have in the bathtub with you,

and I'll try to sing all the songs that you've taught me.

And when I can talk, I'll tell you that I'm sorry for the time
that I pulled your ear really hard.

And *I'll* tell you that it was an accident when I tore the painting you brought home from school.

When I can talk, I'll tell you how wonderful I think you are.

And I'll let you know that when I grow up
I want to be just like you.

I can't talk now, but when I do,
the thing I'll want to say most of all is

I love you.

E
MAR

I Can't Talk Yet, but When I Do . . .
Text copyright © 2003 by Julie Markes
Illustrations copyright © 2003 by Laura Rader
Manufactured in China. All rights reserved.
www.harperchildrens.com

Library of Congress Cataloging-in-Publication Data
Markes, Julie.
I can't talk yet, but when I do . . . / by Julie Markes ; illustrated by Laura Rader. 1st ed.
p. cm.
Summary: A baby recites the benefits of having an older sibling for sharing, fun, and love.
ISBN 0-06-009921-6—ISBN 0-06-009922-4 (lib. bdg.)
[1. Babies—Fiction. 2. Brothers and sisters—Fiction.] I. Rader, Laura, ill. II. Title.
PZ7.M339454 Iae 2003
[E] —dc21   2002005642
CIP
AC

Typography by Stephanie Bart-Horvath
1 2 3 4 5 6 7 8 9 10
❖
First Edition